Sherlock Holmes and the Curious Adventure of the Clockwork Prince

A Victorian Romp

by Cleve Haubold
Music by James Alfred Hitt

A SAMUEL FRENCH ACTING EDITION

SAMUEL FRENCH

FOUNDED 1830

New York Hollywood London Toronto

SAMUELFRENCH.COM

DEDICATION

This piece is affectionately dedicated to the memorable words and music of Sir Arthur Conan Doyle, Sir William Gilbert and Sir Arthur Sullivan for the endless hours of joy which they give.

PRODUCTION NOTES

The soundest advice for the successful performance of this piece is still Sir William S. Gilbert's sage comment on the acting of comedy:

"It is absolutely essential to the success of this piece that it should be played with the most perfect seriousness and gravity throughout. There should be no exaggeration in costume, make-up or demeanour; and the characters, one and all, should appear to believe, throughout, in the perfect sincerity of their words and actions. Directly the actors show that they are conscious of the absurdity of their utterances, the piece begins to drag."

THE MUSIC FOR THIS PLAY COMPOSED BY JAMES ALFRED HITT IS AVAILABLE FOR PURCHASE FROM SAMUEL FRENCH, INC. AT A FEE OF $11.00 PLUS POSTAGE.

CHARACTERS

BRIGHTON, the butler

LUCY
MELISSA } Maids
JANE

MRS. ALAN, the cook

SIR SULLIVAN SINISTER, a professional villain

SIR GILBERT MALLOW, the Marshmallow King

BERTRAM MALLOW, his son, The Clockwork Prince

DR. JOHN WATSON

SHERLOCK HOLMES

LACKEYS, FOOTMEN, HOUSEMAIDS and
STABLE-BOYS to taste.

Sherlock Holmes and the Curious Adventure of the Clockwork Prince

SETTING: *The elegant drawing room of* SIR GILBERT MALLOW's *town house in London on New Year's Eve, 1899. The "Front Parlour Fancy" stage setting beloved by the Victorian theatre will serve nicely.*

The OVERTURE plays. The CURTAINS OPEN—red velvet, of course—as the MUSIC VAMPS. The grandfather clock strikes 10:30. The double doors to the hall fly open, flooding the room with light. BRIGHTON, *the Perfect English Butler, strides into the room. He is the dour master of all he surveys, except when he is taking orders. He moves swiftly around the room, turning up the gaslight, which reflects from the cut glass of the chandeliers and the gleaming woodwork.* BRIGHTON *compares his pocket watch with the grandfather clock, steps to the hall door and claps his hands but once. That is all that* BRIGHTON *needs to do.*

BRIGHTON. Girls . . . if you please . . . Miss Lucy . . . ?

(MISS LUCY, *a maid, enters and curtseys, then takes up her position of attention.* LUCY *is 16, pert and charming.*)

LUCY. Yes, Mister Brighton.
BRIGHTON. Miss Melissa . . . ?

(MELISSA, *another maid, enters, curtseys and takes up her*

7

position. She is 39—and has been for several years.
She is a thin, spinsterish sort.)

MELISSA. Yes, Mister Brighton.
BRIGHTON. (*Rolling his eyes to heaven for the patience*
he will need with JANE.) Miss Jane . . . ?

(JANE, *a maid, enters, curtseys, nearly falls, but is caught*
by the other maids. JANE *is a plump, short, jolly sort of*
32 years. She is not terribly efficient, but has the best
of intentions.)

JANE. (*Giggling.*) Mister Brighton.
BRIGHTON. (*Correcting.*) *Yes,* Mister Brighton.
JANE. Yes, Sir.
BRIGHTON. (*Long-suffering.*) A lass . . . a lass . . .
and a *lack*.
JANE. Yes, Sir!
BRIGHTON. And where is Mrs. Alan, the cook?
MAIDS. Not here, Mister Brighton.
BRIGHTON. Precisely the cause of my inquiry. We shall
carry on without her. (*Taking a stance.*) As you are doubt-
lessly aware, tonight we are upon the very eve of the New
Century.
MAIDS. Yes, Mister Brighton.
BRIGHTON. And from the extensive preparations below
stairs, you must have noticed that this is the date of young
Bertram Mallow's annual birthday celebration.
MAIDS. Yes, Mister Brighton.
BRIGHTON. And . . . as you must also have noticed
. . . Bertram is the son and only heir of our employer, Sir
Gilbert Mallow.
MAIDS. Yes, Mister Brighton.
BRIGHTON. And . . . as is common knowledge . . .
this is the date upon which young Bertram Mallow will

attain his seniority. He comes of age at the stroke of midnight.

LUCY. (*Brightly.*) What's that mean, Mister Brighton?

BRIGHTON. He will turn twenty-one.

LUCY. Oh . . . Thank you, Mister Brighton.

BRIGHTON. All of these tidbits of information are surely common knowledge throughout the household . . .

MAIDS. Yes, Mister Brighton.

BRIGHTON. . . . But I thought it well to mention them again at this particular time.

MAIDS. Thank you, Mister Brighton.

BRIGHTON. 'Tis a time for merry song.

MAIDS. Yes, Mister Brighton.

BRIGHTON. For feasting and enjoyment.

MAIDS. Yes, Mister Brighton.

BRIGHTON. And you'll be festive as you're told . . . to keep in your employment.

MAIDS. Thank you, Mister Brighton.

BRIGHTON. (*Consulting his pocket watch.*) And now it is time that we *heard* some festivity . . . and *saw* some employment!

MAIDS. Yes, Mister Brighton. Thank you, Mister Brighton.

BRIGHTON. (*Raising an imperious finger.*) Commence.

MALLOW MENIALS' MERRY MELODY

(*The* MAIDS *whip out mops, brooms, buckets and polishing cloths, and begin to sing as they put up decorations and clean the already immaculate drawing room.*)

MAIDS.
'Tis a time for merry song,
    For feasting and enjoyment.
We'll be festive as we're told,
    To keep in our employment!

BRIGHTON. (*Singing.*)
Polish silver,
Dust the chairs,
    And sweep for all you're worth! May
Everything be
Sparkling bright
    For Bertram Mallow's birthday!
    MAIDS.
Everything *is*
Sparkling bright
    For Bertram Mallow's birthday!

(*They dance and clean a bit.*)

MAIDS.
This is such a holiday!
    The halls are decked, so therefore,
We shall laugh and smile and sing,
    Though we don't know the wherefore.
    BRIGHTON.
Shine the crystal!
Wax the floors!
    And when you've all that fun done,
Put out little
Paper horns
    For New Year's Eve in London!
    MAIDS.
We've *put* out little paper horns
For New Year's Eve in London!

(*They clean and dance a bit.*)

MAIDS.
We're told this New Year's Eve will end
    All eighteen-ninety-nine scenes.
We can't wait till twelve o'clock,
    To find what Greenwich Mean means.

BRIGHTON.
Beat the carpets.
Set the gaslight
   To the proper shading,
To suit a Birthday
Party, New Year's
   Eve with masquerading!
   MAIDS.
We'd like a Birthday Party, New Year's
Eve with masquerading!

(They dance and clean until the MUSIC ends. The hall doors burst open. MRS. ALAN enters. She is 60, a deaf but agile cook with an ear-trumpet.)

MAIDS. *(Together.)* Mrs. Alan, the cook!

BRIGHTON. I cannot tell you how delighted I am that you recognize Mrs. Alan, the cook. She has only been employed in this household for forty years.

MRS. ALAN. *(Holding her ear trumpet.)* Am I early? It was so quiet that I thought no one was here.

BRIGHTON. *(Holding out his watch.)* Mrs. Alan . . . Where have you been?

MRS. ALAN. *(Peering at the watch.)* Oh . . . about ten-thirty.

BRIGHTON. *(To the MAIDS.)* Girls . . . get about your employments.

MAIDS. *(Curtseying.)* Yes, Mister Brighton . . . *(They gather up their cleaning paraphernalia and exit.)*

BRIGHTON. *(Calling after them.)* And see to it that you *are* festive. Now, Mrs. Alan, I think that we must have a word about dinner for this auspicious occasion.

MRS. ALAN. *(With a slight cough.)* Oh, it's only a slight chill.

BRIGHTON. The menu for dinner!

MRS. ALAN. How thoughtful of you, Mister Brighton. I

will wrap a bit of flannel about my throat to keep out the night air . . . First thing in the morning.

BRIGHTON. (*Trying to speak clearly into the ear trumpet, but* MRS. ALAN *moves it with every turn.*) Have you written out the menu for dinner?

MRS. ALAN. It is kind of you to be so concerned about my health, but I really must write out the menu for dinner. (*She goes to the desk and picks up a large folded piece of paper and a pencil.*)

BRIGHTON. Thank heavens!

MRS. ALAN. Oh . . . since last Tuesday, as I recall. (*She begins to jot down menu items as she moves about the room.*)

(*A SPRING BELL jingles in the hall.*)

BRIGHTON. Excuse me a moment, Mrs. Alan. That would be Sir Gilbert ringing for me.

MRS. ALAN. What a good idea! We could serve those with cheese. (*She devotes her total attention, such as it is, to making notes.*)

BRIGHTON. (*Trying to be heard.*) Carry on with the menu! I am going now! I shall be back in a moment! (*He exits.*)

MRS. ALAN. Oh, no. One never serves raspberry jam with licorice marshmallows.

MRS. ALAN'S MENU-ET

(*As the music begins, a figure dressed in a black hooded cape steals into the room. He dims the gaslight and proceeds to break into the secret drawer of the desk, making a great deal of noise with crowbars, a large hammer and spectacular explosive charges. Naturally* MRS. ALAN *does not hear him. When a particularly loud attack on the desk draws her momentary attention, the figure darts into hiding behind the draperies, under the desk or behind a chair. Even in the dim light, we can see the black waxed moustache and gleaming monocle which mark the intruder as* SIR SULLIVAN SINISTER. *No one recognizes him at this point because, of course, we have never seen him before in our lives. During her song he extracts a large brass key from a tin box in the desk and replaces it with a folded paper, closed with sealing wax. He returns the tin box to its hiding place and slips away with the stolen key. He thoughtfully turns up the gaslight as the song ends.*)

MRS. ALAN. (*Singing.*)
First in the group comes a savoury soup,
    Cooked with grunions, Spanish onions,
And noodles that loop.
    (SIR SULLIVAN *makes a small noise that is not noticed by* MRS. ALAN.)
A salad that muffles objections with truffles
    Has in each pitted peach
Mounds of Roquefort . . . one scoop!

(SIR SULLIVAN *attacks the desk with a crowbar.*)

MRS. ALAN. (*Speaking.*) Goodness me . . . Why, what was that? Very like it was the cat . . . We used to have a cat . . .
    MRS. ALAN. (*Singing.*)
Next a delicious selection of fishes,
    Pickled herring beyond bearing
Surpasses your wishes.
    (SIR SULLIVAN *beats at the desk with a large hammer . . . unnoticed.*)
There are platters stacked high with ham, steaming hot
    racks of lamb,
    Embellished with relish,
Served on Blue Willow dishes.

(SIR SULLIVAN *sets off a mild explosive charge.*)

MRS. ALAN. (*Speaking.*) Lo, what light through yonder
window breaks? It is the east . . . or maybe not.
MRS. ALAN. (*Singing.*)
Then as a sweet if you want more to eat,
    There is candy, soaked in brandy,
Burning blue from the heat.
    (SIR SULLIVAN *steals the key, leaves the ransom note and
    slams the tin box back into the secret drawer of the desk.*)
And then you can take a big serving of cake.
    You'll be slicing sugar icing
For a true baker's treat!

(SIR SULLIVAN *scurries out, slamming the door behind him.
    Instantly the hall doors are flung open.* BRIGHTON *en-
    ters, followed by* SIR GILBERT MALLOW *and* BERTRAM
    MALLOW, *his son.*)

BRIGHTON. (*Announcing.*) Sir Gilbert Mallow and young
Master Bertram.
MRS. ALAN. (*To* BRIGHTON.) I knew you'd like it.
SIR GILBERT. That will be all, Brighton.
BRIGHTON. Thank you, Sir. Come, Mrs. Alan . . .
MRS. ALAN. (*Crossing with* BRIGHTON *to the door.*) Oh,
Sir Gilbert . . . ! (*Curtseys.*) Master Bertram . . . !
Where's the cat . . . ?
BRIGHTON. (*Leading her out.*) We do not keep a cat.
MRS. ALAN. Oh . . . the poor thing. I'll send a wreath.

(BRIGHTON *and* MRS. ALAN *exit.* SIR GILBERT *looks around
    cautiously and closes the door.*)

SIR GILBERT. Bertram, my boy, I suppose you are aware
of the occasion for tonight's festivities?
BERTRAM. Yes, Father . . .

SIR GILBERT. (*Stifling a sob.*) Father . . . ! Yes . . . yes . . .

BERTRAM. (*Puzzled.*) Yes, Father. (*Rattling on proudly.*) This is December 31, 1899, the last day of the old century. At precisely twelve o'clock the year will be 1900 and I shall be 21 years of age. The time is exactly 10:47. That clock is three minutes slow and the chimes don't work properly. People are forever remarking on how good I am at always knowing the correct time. Would you like to hear me imitate a music box on my teeth?

SIR GILBERT. (*Controlling a grave emotion.*) Not just now . . . Bertram . . . It is time that I must tell you a story.

BERTRAM. The time now is exactly 10:48.

SIR GILBERT. Bertram!

BERTRAM. Sorry.

SIR GILBERT. For twenty-one long years, I have held this secret in my heart. I have found no easy way to reveal it to you . . . so I shall be direct. (*A hand on* BERTRAM'S *shoulder.*) My son . . . you are *clockwork!*

BERTRAM. (*Pause.*) My father . . . you are *crackers!*

SIR GILBERT. It is not unnatural that you should say that. But wait until you have heard the entire story.

BERTRAM. I like stories. May I sit in your lap?

SIR GILBERT. No.

BERTRAM. (*Sitting in a chair.*) Oh . . .

(*The grandfather clock chimes the three-quarter hour—Westminster chimes.*)

SIR GILBERT. Bertram, stop that!

BERTRAM. It wasn't me . . . it was . . . (*Pointing to clock.*)

SIR GILBERT. Forgive me, Bertram. I am wrought. Indeed am *over*wrought. (*Pulling himself and a stiff glass of sherry together.*) Long ago—on a chill winter's night such as this—you were found on my doorstep. You were but an infant, slumbering in a tin bread-box . . . long ago. Long, long ago.

BERTRAM. How long?

SIR GILBERT. Oh . . . about sixteen inches—your ordinary tin bread-box. Your swaddling clothes were knit of steel wool. Your only toy . . . a large brass key with the operating instructions: "Wind fully each New Year's Eve. On Leap Year, give it an extra quarter-turn."

BERTRAM. Then I was . . . ?

SIR GILBERT. A clockwork foundling. I was childless. I had no heir. I welcomed you to my arms, although in your youth, you had a tendency to rattle.

BERTRAM. But . . . How did I grow?

SIR GILBERT. I suppose it was managed in the usual fashion . . . India-rubber bands . . . lazy tongs . . . concealed springs. They were very fashionable in the late 70's . . . especially at Maskelyne and Cooke's magic theatre in Egyptian Hall.

BERTRAM. Then that accounts for . . . (*Touching his chest.*)

SIR GILBERT. Yes . . . the keyhole in your chest.

BERTRAM. You always said it was a birthmark. A hollow birthmark.

SIR GILBERT. Only to protect you until you were old enough to understand.

BERTRAM. I thought *everybody* had a hollow birthmark. I never asked around.

SIR GILBERT. Nor need you ever! At the stroke of midnight, you become heir to the Mallow family fortune! I worked my way up from lowly Mallow Marsh in the North of England, to build a financial kingdom upon the solid foundation of . . . Marshmallows!

BERTRAM. Marshmallows! Hear, hear!

SIR GILBERT. Marshmallow plantations in Saigon and Caracas! Marshmallow packaging plants in London, New

York and Paris! Corporately owned Marshmallow shops throughout the civilized world . . . and in the American state of Nebraska!

BERTRAM. Bravo!

SIR GILBERT. And to guarantee your success in the New Century, I have devised for you a legacy of boundless worth . . .

BERTRAM. Yes, Sir . . . ?

SIR GILBERT. The closely guarded—the only copy in the universe—the secret recipe for *Licorice* Marshmallows! Worth millions!

BERTRAM. Should be delicious with raspberry jam!

SIR GILBERT. This is the culmination of all my desires. I am the undisputed Marshmallow King . . . and you . . . Bertram . . . (*Reaching a peak of filial emotion.*) are my Clockwork Prince!

BERTRAM. My . . . uhh . . .

SIR GILBERT. Call me *Father!*

BERTRAM. My Father!

SIR GILBERT. My Son! (*They embrace. It is a moment of family devotion too beautiful for words.*) Now, for the winding.

BERTRAM. I must confess . . . I am feeling a bit run down.

SIR GILBERT. Not to worry, Bertram. Since that blessed day that you came to run . . . er . . . to *live* in this house, I have kept that large brass key securely locked in a tin box in the secret drawer of my desk. (*Crosses to desk.*) Except, of course, for the annual windings.

BERTRAM. (*Weakening.*) It's 10:57.

SIR GILBERT. (*Indicating each.*) The desk . . . the secret drawer . . . the tin box . . . the large brass key . . .

BERTRAM. Yes, Father?

SIR GILBERT. The large brass key . . .

BERTRAM. And *you* said it was a hollow birthmark.

SIR GILBERT. (*With horrible realization.*) The . . . large . . . brass . . . key . . .

BERTRAM. (*Sensing something amiss.*) The large brass key . . . ?

SIR GILBERT. The large brass key . . . is *gone* . . . *Gone* . . . ! *GONE* . . . !

BERTRAM. (*Sitting and feeling his pulse.*) I suppose this means I don't get the Marshmallow Company.

SIR GILBERT. (*Excitedly.*) Bertram, sound the alarm! (BERTRAM *rises and presses his nose.* BERTRAM *begins to ring loudly like an alarm clock.*) Bertram, stop that!

BERTRAM. (*Stops ringing.*) Would you rather I did Westminster chimes . . . ? (*Reaching for his ear.*)

SIR GILBERT. (*Tugging at the bell cord.*) Brighton! Brighton!

BERTRAM. (*Helpfully indicating his other ear.*) Big Ben? (*Since he is being ignored, he sits, presses his ear and chimes softly to himself.*)

SIR GILBERT. (*Running to the hall doors and flinging them open.*) Brighton!

(BRIGHTON *rushes in, followed by* MRS. ALAN, *who rushes as best she can.*)

BRIGHTON. Sir Gilbert! What is amiss?

SIR GILBERT. This is no time for riddles! We have been pilfered!

BRIGHTON. (*Shocked.*) No, Sir . . . !

SIR GILBERT. (*Running about.*) Yes, Sir! Pilfered, Sir! Robbed, Sir! Burgled, Sir! Plundered, Sir! And other expressions, Sir, synonymous with the unlawful loss of property, Sir!

BRIGHTON. Yes, Sir.

SIR GILBERT. Rally the staff! Rally everyone. Fetch every key in the house. Lock every door and window. Lock every cupboard and clothespress! Lock every nook and cranny! The thief must not escape!

BRIGHTON. (*At the door.*) Yes, Sir. At once, Sir. May I ask, Sir, what has been stolen?

SIR GILBERT. A large brass key!

BRIGHTON. Yes, Sir. A large brass key, Sir. May I ask, Sir, what does the large brass key *fit?*

SIR GILBERT. It . . . I . . . A large brass *keyhole!* Now be off with you!

BRIGHTON. Yes, Sir. (*Hurries out clapping his hands.*) Miss Lucy! Miss Melissa! Miss Jane! Everyone. Hurry! Hurry!

SIR GILBERT. (*Crossing to* MRS. ALAN.) I have a matter of the utmost urgency for you to perform, Madam, if you feel that you are equal to the task!

MRS. ALAN. (*She does not hear one blessed word he says, but she smiles and nods amiably.*) Oh, yes, Sir. Yes.

SIR GILBERT. You are to hurry—as fast as you are able— into the next street and to fetch the one man in all of London capable of solving this mystery. Naturally you know of whom I speak.

MRS. ALAN. (*Smiling and nodding.*) Oh, yes, Sir. Oh, yes . . .

SIR GILBERT. Wisely said. Wisely said! The man to whom I refer is, of course, none other than Mr. *Sherlock Holmes!*

MRS. ALAN. Yes . . . Oh, yes, Sir.

SIR GILBERT. You are to bring him here immediately. Do not listen to a word from Mrs. Hudson, his housekeeper . . .

MRS. ALAN. (*Not hearing a word from him.*) Oh, no, Sir.

SIR GILBERT. Do not listen to a word from Dr. Watson, his friend . . .

MRS. ALAN. Oh, no, Sir.

SIR GILBERT. He lodges at 221B Baker Street.

MRS. ALAN. Oh, yes, Sir.

SIR GILBERT. Do you have all of that . . . ? (*She nods.*) Mr. Sherlock Holmes . . . (*Nods.*) You will find him in *Baker Street!*

MRS. ALAN. Yes, Sir. (*Crosses to the door.*) Just one small question, Sir . . .

SIR GILBERT. Yes . . . ?

MRS. ALAN. Would you like that *with* or *without* mint sauce? (SIR GILBERT *stands suddenly dumbfounded.* MRS. ALAN *crosses to him and places a small wreath with black ribbons into his hand. She pats his hand sympathetically as he stands open-mouthed.*) For the cat . . . Poor thing. (*She crosses to door.*)

SIR GILBERT. (*Recovering at the top of his lungs.*) Find him in *Baker Street!*

MRS. ALAN. (*At the door—smiling as she wraps a bit of flannel about her throat against the night air.*) Baker Street. (*Exits, mumbling to herself.*) Baker Street . . . Yes . . . in Baker Street . . .

SIR GILBERT. (*Crossing to* BERTRAM, *who quickly and inconspicuously stops chiming to himself.*) My son . . .

BERTRAM. Yes, Father . . . ?

SIR GILBERT. (*Sympathetically.*) I know what you must be thinking.

BERTRAM. Yes, Father . . . If we cannot find the key . . .

SIR GILBERT. (*Holding back a sob.*) Yes, my son . . . ?

BERTRAM. If we cannot find the key at *all* . . .

SIR GILBERT. Yes . . . ?

BERTRAM. . . . May I open my birthday presents *early?*

(SIR GILBERT *flings the cat's funeral wreath into the fireplace and steadies himself against the mantel to regain his composure.* BERTRAM *chimes once, very softly to himself. This tender scene is immediately shattered as all the doors to the drawing room fly open.* BRIGHTON, *the maids* LUCY, MELISSA *and* JANE, *and any additional* LACKEYS, FOOTMEN, KITCHEN-MAIDS *and* STABLE-BOYS *bound into the room, waving keys of all descriptions. They attempt to lock everything within reach—*

*windows, doors, antimacassars and armoires. As they
fill the room with the ON-KEY SONG, BERTRAM motions LUCY to him and whispers to her. LUCY registers
amazement, but agrees to help him. As each servant
runs past, LUCY exchanges keys with him, and passes
the keys one by one to BERTRAM, who tries them—
without avail—in his keyhole. SIR GILBERT adds to the
confusion by directing the efforts of the household.*

THE ON-KEY SONG

LUCY.
Keys are turning,
Tumblers churning.
   I'm no locksmith, but I'm learning.
   CHORUS OF SERVANTS.
She is quite correct concerning
Lack of locksmiths, but we're learning.

(ALL *try keys in locks.* BERTRAM *motions* LUCY *to him and
    whispers.*)

MELISSA.
Locks I'm trying,
Not denying
   I think keyholes are for spying!
   CHORUS OF SERVANTS.
Shame on you! We are decrying
Thoughts that keyholes are for spying!

(ALL *crouch and peer through keyholes, real and
    imaginary.*)

JANE.
Latches latching,
Catches catching,
   No one's lock and key is matching!

(*She holds up a giant key and a box with a tiny lock.*)

CHORUS OF SERVANTS.
Foil the evil plot that's hatching!
Find the locks with keys a-matching!

(ALL *dance round, trying keys in locks. At the last note of the dance, all the keys fit something as locks click into place all over the house.*)

BRIGHTON. It is done, Sir.
SIR GILBERT. Well done, Brighton. (*There is an authoritative KNOCK at the hall doors.*) It is he! We are saved, saved . . . saved! Brighton . . . the door! I give you England's only unofficial consulting detective . . . Mr. Sherlock Holmes!
ALL. (*Enthusiastically.*) Hip, hip, horray!

(BRIGHTON *opens the hall doors.* SIR SULLIVAN SINISTER *toddles in, cunningly disguised as* MRS. ALAN. *A bit of flannel around the lower part of his face hides his black waxed moustache.*)

SIR SULLIVAN. (*As* MRS. ALAN.) Sir Gilbert, Sir Gilbert . . . Oh, Sir Gilbert . . . We are fresh out of mint sauce.

(SIR SULLIVAN *toddles out.* SIR GILBERT *crosses to the door and peers after him, confused. There is an authoritative KNOCK at the French doors which open onto the balcony.*)

SIR GILBERT. Surely that is he! We are saved, saved . . . saved! Brighton, the French doors! I give you England's only unofficial consulting detective . . . Mr. Sherlock Holmes!

ALL. (*With considerably less enthusiasm.*) Hip, hip, hooray . . .

(BRIGHTON *opens the French doors.* DR. WATSON *bumbles in, laden with satchels and portmanteaus.*)

WATSON. Mmmm . . . Ah . . . Oh, yes . . . The front door was locked, so I climbed the rainspout to the balcony.

SIR GILBERT. What a magnificent disguise!

WATSON. Who . . . ? Oh . . . ? I . . . ?

SIR GILBERT. I am Sir Gilbert Mallow and this is my son, Bertram.

WATSON. (*Presenting a calling card.*) I am Dr. John Watson.

SIR GILBERT. Subtle . . . How very subtle . . . a disguised calling card. (*He passes it round for the others to admire.*) In that false moustache and silly hat, you look a perfect fool. An admirable ruse!

WATSON. (*Helpfully.*) The hat comes off. (*Looking out the French doors.*) I wonder where Holmes has got off to.

(*There is an authoritative KNOCK at the window.*)

SIR GILBERT. (*Tiring.*) Surely that is he . . . and so on. Brighton, the window. I give you England's only . . . and so forth . . . Mr. Sherlock Holmes . . .

ALL. (*With positive apathy.*) Hip, hip, *et cetera* . . .

(BRIGHTON *opens the window.* HOLMES *climbs smartly in. He carries a large satchel and a violin case in addition to his usual accoutrements.*)

WATSON. Jove . . . ! *Holmes* . . . !

HOLMES. You always say that. (*To* SIR GILBERT.) From the perplexed expression on your face and the bits of powdered sugar on your left elbow, I deduce that you are Sir Gilbert Mallow, the Marshmallow King. You have been deep in thought, and will soon take a long voyage across water.

WATSON. Jove, Holmes . . . !

SIR GILBERT. You are truly Sherlock Holmes! (*He attempts to rouse the others to enthusiasm, but they do not rise to the occasion.*) Hip, hip . . . Oh, never mind. Mr. Holmes, for those who may not be familiar with your accomplishments, could you give us a brief resume?

HOLMES. Unnecessary. But it is entirely possible that I may be able to recall to mind some few noteworthy triumphs with which I have been remotely connected. Watson . . . the notebook . . .

(WATSON *takes from a satchel a huge scrapbook, bulging with clippings and pamphlets. He passes it to* HOLMES.)

HOLMES' SUITE

HOLMES. (*Singing.*)

I've monographs on "Chronographs and Clockwork" I've collected.

I've papers too on Irish stew and goulash I've inspected.

I've made a dogged catalog of all tobacco ashes.

I've studied hands and Speckled Bands and hidden treasure caches.

CHORUS. (ALL.)

He's studied hands and Speckled Bands and hidden treasure caches!

HOLMES.

Moriarty! He was to me a villain most resented.

I tracked him down and then I found Moriarty demented!

I trace rich uncles, Blue Carbuncles, study life that's seamier.

I also solved a case involving Scandal in Bohemia!

CHORUS.

He also solved a case involving Scandal in Bohemia!

HOLMES.

I've proved it odd that old Lestrade, the Scotland Yard
     detective,

Can't solve a case to save his face. His logic is defective.

I look for clues on dead men's shoes. I must have found a
     million.

I even found a haunting hound, who turned out Basker-
     villian!

CHORUS.

He even found a haunting hound, who turned out Basker-
     villian!

HOLMES.

The Sign of Four was such a boring case, although I said it

At the time was more a crime than League for the Red-
     Headed.

If my conjecture is correct, you have a *worthy* riddle.

Till time is ripe, I'll smoke my pipe and play upon my
     fiddle!

CHORUS.

Till time is ripe, he'll smoke his pipe and play upon his
     fiddle!

(HOLMES *improvises a brief, lively country dance to which
     the* MAIDS *perform decorous dances suited to the
     drawing-room.*)

WATSON. (*Speaking.*) Jove, Holmes . . . You know
what I always say . . .

HOLMES. (*Less than pleased.*) You always say, "Jove,
Holmes . . ."

WATSON. I always say, "Be he ever so humble, there's
no police like Holmes!"

HOLMES. (*Glowering.*) I'd rather you said, "Jove,
Holmes . . . " (*The grandfather clock strikes the hour*

of eleven. Without consulting a watch.) It is precisely 11:03. That clock is slow . . . and the chimes don't work properly.

SIR GILBERT. Thank you, Mr. Holmes, for coming so promptly in response to my message.

HOLMES. Your message? Hmmm . . . This is a matter which we must discuss with the utmost confidentiality.

SIR GILBERT. We shall be confidential.

ALL THE SERVANTS. (*Gathering around to listen.*) Oh, yes, confidentiality . . . Confidential, yes . . . You may speak confidentially . . . We shall certainly keep it in confidence . . . Etc. . . .

HOLMES. In private.

ALL THE SERVANTS. (*Gathering closer.*) Definitely private . . . We shall keep it private . . . We shall respect your privacy . . . Very private indeed . . . Etc.

HOLMES. (*Meaningfully.*) With only the *essential* parties present!

ALL THE SERVANTS. (*Closer still.*) Of course, only the essential . . . Essential parties only . . . We are very essential . . . Essentially confidential . . . Etc.

HOLMES. (*Motioning the* SERVANTS *out various doors.*) You are not essential . . . You are not essential . . . Non-essential . . . Clearly not essential . . . Not essential at all . . . Essentially non-essential. (THE SERVANTS *exit. To* WATSON.) Definitely not essential . . .

WATSON. (*Hurt.*) Holmes!

HOLMES. Oh . . . very well. You may stay. But only out of habit.

WATSON. (*Mumbling to himself.*) Habit, indeed . . . Hmmmph . . . Well . . .

HOLMES. (*To* SIR GILBERT.) This message was delivered to my lodgings moments ago by an elderly person of the feminine gender with a bit of flannel wrapped around her throat to keep out the night air. I saw her from my window.

SIR GILBERT. Mrs. Alan, my cook.

HOLMES. She thrust this note under the front door, blew a rather festive seasonal hunting call upon her ear-trumpet, then vanished into the night with a speed one could only describe as remarkable for one of her apparent years. She has a mole upon her left eyebrow.

SIR GILBERT. That indeed was she. Although I am surprised at the part about the rather festive seasonal hunting call.

HOLMES. I am surprised at nothing.

BERTRAM. (*Since he and* WATSON *have been left out of things—to* WATSON.) Would you like to hear me imitate a music box on my teeth?

WATSON. Do you know "Flow Gently, Sweet Afton"?

SIR GILBERT. Stop that, Bertram!

HOLMES. Quiet, Watson!

WATSON. (*Subsiding into mumbles.*) Hmmp . . . Well . . . Always a favorite tune of mine . . .

HOLMES. The message reads as follows . . .
"The key to the mystery
Hides in the locks.
Sir Gilbert's—at eleven,
To play mental blocks.
        Best regards of the Season,
            Your obedient Servant, Etc. . . .
                Sir Sullivan Sinister"

SIR GILBERT. Sir Sullivan Sinister . . . ?

HOLMES. See for yourself. (*Shows* GILBERT *the note.*)

SIR GILBERT. That is *not* my hand!

HOLMES. No. It is a note.

SIR GILBERT. Who is this Sir Sullivan Sinister?

HOLMES. A former actor of great talent, who went to the bad . . . as many of them do. He currently finds employment as a criminal. I have encountered him before. He is a master of disguise . . . subtle . . . devious . . . (*In a terrifying whisper.*) He is *nemesis!*

SIR GILBERT. We are Church of England . . .

HOLMES. Obviously. This is not your message, and yet you sent for me on a matter of some urgency . . . If I judge correctly from the deep heel-prints in the carpet . . . and the remnants of a cat funeral wreath smouldering in the fireplace.

SIR GILBERT. You judge correctly.

HOLMES. Of course. Please state your problem concisely. I should like to be back in Baker Street before the turn of the century. I have a little red and white paper horn there which I have been saving to celebrate the occasion.

SIR GILBERT. We have little paper horns in assorted colours here, but I shall respect your wishes. (HOLMES *moves about the room, examining things through his magnifying glass.*) To put it concisely . . . This is my son, Bertram. He is made of clockwork. If he is not wound each New Year's Eve, he will run down. We might find some use for him as a halltree or a paper-weight if he expires in a suitable posture . . . but . . . but (*With emotion.*) I had higher plans for his future.

HOLMES. (*Absently examining a glass paperweight with a snow scene inside it.*) Seems to be no problem there . . . Look, Watson, it snows when you turn it upside down.

WATSON. So it does.

SIR GILBERT. But the large brass key that winds him has been stolen . . . stolen . . . (*Sits—in a highly emotional state and a leather armchair.*) Stolen . . .

HOLMES. (*Stiffening with the realization.*) Clockwork . . . ? Did you say *clockwork?* (*Peers closely at* SIR GILBERT.)

SIR GILBERT. Some moments ago.

HOLMES. Watson, did he say *clockwork?*

WATSON. Sorry, Holmes. I wasn't listening. (*To* SIR GILBERT.) Where could I buy one of these paperweights?

SIR GILBERT. At Hamley Brothers . . . fourth floor rear.

HOLMES. Clockwork . . . ?

BERTRAM. He said clockwork. (*Proudly presses his nose and rings like an alarm clock.*)

HOLMES. (*Springing into action and listening at* BERTRAM's *chest.*) Hmmm . . . Were it not for my reputation, I should almost be surprised. Sir Gilbert, it is fortunate that you did send for me. Quick, Watson . . . the satchel. We haven't a minute to lose.

BERTRAM. (*Feeling his pulse.*) I think I've already lost about *half* a minute.

HOLMES. Look in the compartment marked "Large Brass Key."

WATSON. I have the compartment. Jove, Holmes . . . there's a large brass key in it.

HOLMES. Quickly . . . give it here.

SIR GILBERT. We are saved . . . saved . . . Saved!

(HOLMES *tries the key in* BERTRAM's *chest.*)

BERTRAM. That tickles!

HOLMES. Drat! Almost, but not quite. It doesn't fit!

SIR GILBERT. We are lost . . . lost . . . lost! (*Crosses to desk and sits.*)

HOLMES. (*Returning his key to* WATSON—*speaking to* SIR GILBERT.) Where did you keep your large brass key?

SIR GILBERT. In this secret drawer of my desk . . . In this tin box. But it is empty . . . empty . . . ! (*A large folded paper, closed with sealing wax falls out of the tin box.*) Well . . . almost empty.

HOLMES. (*Pouncing upon the paper and the tin box.*) Hmmm . . . Marks of a Number Five-Seventeen Patent Vandercleve Heavy-Duty Crow-Bar. Aha . . . ! The faint odour of Three-Quarter Strength Clapsaddle Blasting Powder. From the Hamburg Factory, I should judge. Oho . . . ! (*Opening the folded paper.*) Near-microscopic traces of cigar ash . . . obviously Turkish Latakia in an exclusive blend found only at the one-eyed tobacconist's shop on High Street in Bideford, Devon! West side of the street. This robbery is clearly the work of Sir Sullivan Sinister!

BERTRAM. (*Peering over* HOLMES's *shoulder*.) He signed his name to the note.

HOLMES. (*Petulantly holding the note away from* BERTRAM.) I would have known anyway.

WATSON. What does it say?

HOLMES. (*Reading—as if it were going to be a rhyme*.)
"To save the clockwork
  Youth named Bertram,
  To the cloakroom in Victoria Station before midnight,
  Deliver the secret recipe for Licorice Marshmallows.
              Best regards . . . etc. . . .
                  Sir Sullivan . . . etc. . . .

WATSON. That's dreadful . . .

SIR GILBERT. Yes . . . Dreadful . . .

WATSON. It doesn't even rhyme.

BERTRAM. (*Helpfully*.) It's very hard to find a proper rhyme for Licorice Marshmallows.

HOLMES. (*Insistently*.) He needn't have signed it, you know. I *would* have *known!*

SIR GILBERT. Then there is only one thing to do!

HOLMES. Uh . . . I suppose so . . . Yes . . . What . . . ?

SIR GILBERT. To save Bertram, we must give Sir Sullivan Sinister the secret recipe for Licorice Marshmallows, although it will ruin my son's prospects for the future. On the other hand, if we do not get the large brass key, his prospects for the future are decidedly none too bright.

BERTRAM. Either way I don't get the Marshmallow Company.

WATSON. (*Comforting* BERTRAM.) There, there, my boy. Watch the pretty snowstorm in the paperweight and put your trust in Sherlock Holmes.

HOLMES. Trust me, Sir Gilbert. I shall recover the key

and bring Sir Sullivan Sinister to justice. (*Drifting off.*) And then Watson will write it up very prettily in his memoirs— getting a nice advance royalty, which we always share— and justice will triumph! Eventually.

SIR GILBERT. (*Dashing to his desk.*) No! I am off to Victoria Station with this . . . laundry list . . . (*He picks up another paper.*) Greengrocer's bill . . . (*Another paper.*) Railway timetable . . . (*In desperation he sits at the desk and clutches his head.*) The recipe is . . . We are . . .

HOLMES. I know . . . Gone, gone, gone . . . Lost, lost, lost. Now the time is at hand and the game is afoot!

WATSON. (*Writing in his notebook.*) Could I have that again, Holmes?

HOLMES. Later, Watson. You all *see,* but you do not *observe!* It is evident to me that Sir Sullivan Sinister does not yet *have* the recipe he demands or else he would not have left this note *demanding* the recipe!

BERTRAM. Jove, Mr. Holmes . . . !

HOLMES. Quiet, Watson!

WATSON. (*Mumbling.*) It was him . . . It wasn't me . . . I didn't say it.

HOLMES. The house is securely locked and bolted?

SIR GILBERT. Every lock.

BERTRAM. Every bolt.

HOLMES. I deduced that from the fact we had to enter by means of an icy rainspout, now utterly impassible. Sir Sullivan Sinister is trapped. He cannot escape me this time. (*Crosses to window.*) I took care before I entered to see that the house was surrounded by the Baker Street Irregulars! Come and see! (ALL *go to windows.*)

SIR GILBERT. Baker Street Irregulars . . . ? I see no police . . .

HOLMES. Nor would anyone else. You see that ordinary-looking newsboy across the street? And the boot-black under the gaslight . . . ?

WATSON. I don't think the newsboy is one of the Irregulars, Holmes. I've never seen *him* before.

BERTRAM. What about that *other* ordinary-looking newsboy down at the corner?

HOLMES. No . . . no. He's a stranger to me. It's definitely the newsboy across the street.

SIR GILBERT. The two lads building the snowman . . . ?

HOLMES. I recognize *them*. So the house is completely surrounded by the two lads building the snowman, one or the other of the ordinary-looking newsboys, and quite possibly the boot-black standing under the gaslight. There are others so inconspicuous as to escape all notice. (*He abruptly closes the draperies.*)

WATSON. I'm not sure about either of the newsboys . . .

HOLMES. (*Rapidly changing the subject.*) Now is the time for action, not talk. Sir Gilbert, proceed in perfect certainty with plans for tonight's celebration. I give you my word that I shall unmask Sir Sullivan Sinister and recover the Large Brass Key *and* the recipe for Licorice Marshmallows before the stroke of midnight—since I dislike having matters drag on from one century into the next. Go now! Watson and I have work to do!

SIR GILBERT. Thank you, Mr. Holmes. I cannot tell you what you have done for my confidence. Come, Bertram.

BERTRAM. Can I take one present with me to open now . . . just in case . . . ?

SIR GILBERT. Play with the paperweight. Mr. Holmes . . . Dr. Watson . . . (BERTRAM *and* SIR GILBERT *exit.*)

HOLMES. (*To* WATSON.) What do you mean . . . you're not sure about the newsboy across the street! And in front of a client!

WATSON. Sorry, Holmes.

HOLMES. No time for emotion. (HOLMES *strides about*

the room, his mind racing.) Hmmm . . . Yes . . . Yes
. . . No . . . Perhaps . . . yes . . . yes . . . YES!
The case is as good as solved.

WATSON. Holmes, you really are an automaton—a calcu-
lating machine. There is something positively inhuman in
you at times.

HOLMES. Thank you. Watson, if you please, open satchel
number three . . . and take out the contents of compartment 8-B, subtitle: Disguises.

WATSON. (*Taking out the dress.*) It's a quick-change
costume for a cook. (*Chuckles.*) Who's going to wear that
silly-looking thing?

HOLMES. (*Pause.*) You are.

WATSON. Really, Holmes . . .

HOLMES. The memoirs . . . ? The advance royalties
. . . ?

WATSON. (*Getting into the costume.*) Button me up.

HOLMES. You are to assume the character of Mrs. Alan,
the cook. There is an ear-trumpet in compartment 8-C. And
a bit of flannel to keep out the night air and hide your
moustache. Thus arrayed, you can move freely about the
house, observing everything and reporting back to me.

WATSON. Sounds simple enough.

HOLMES. I shall also be in disguise.

WATSON. (*Foreseeing great difficulties.*) Oh . . .

HOLMES. I may disguise myself as several people . . .
not, however, simultaneously. Some few things are beyond
even *my* talents.

WATSON. How shall I know you?

HOLMES. Therein lies the subtlety. You won't!

WATSON. Clever . . . clever, but confusing.

HOLMES. You will not recognize me . . . and neither
will my old opponent, Sir Sullivan Sinister. This may be the
chance to try out my Cantonese Salad-Chef disguise.

WATSON. That one always fools me.

HOLMES. If the fit is upon me, I may even disguise myself as a grandfather clock!

WATSON. Striking!

HOLMES. Every quarter-hour . . . Westminster chimes! Now, go, Watson . . . And report back at intervals.

WATSON. Report . . . but to whom?

HOLMES. (*Gleefully*.) Aha! One never knows! Therein lies the sport! Go! (WATSON *exits.* HOLMES *crosses to the bell cord and tugs at it to summon the butler. Musing at the bell cord.*) These things can be positively dangerous. Snakes crawl down them. (*A door opens.* SIR SULLIVAN SINISTER *enters, disguised as* MRS. ALAN, *so he looks very much like* WATSON *disguised as* MRS. ALAN.) There you are, Brighton. I want you to . . . (*Peeved.*) Watson, I told you to report back to me at *intervals*.

SIR SULLIVAN. (*As* MRS. ALAN—*averting his face.*) Yes . . . Oh, yes, Sir.

HOLMES. Forty-three seconds is *not* an interval! Aha! I hear the butler approaching. Quickly, Watson, into the clock! (*Pushing* SIR SULLIVAN *toward the grandfather clock.*)

SIR SULLIVAN. Oh, yes, Sir . . . Yes.

HOLMES. And do get the voice right. It's a little higher. (*In a cracked falsetto.*) "Yes, yes . . . Oh, yes, Sir."

SIR SULLIVAN. (*A little higher.*) Yes, yes . . . Oh, yes . . .

HOLMES. Work on it. (*Shuts* SIR SULLIVAN *into the grandfather clock as* BRIGHTON *enters.*)

BRIGHTON. Mr. Holmes . . . ?

HOLMES. I was just examining this antique time-piece for clues.

SIR SULLIVAN. (*From inside the clock.*) Yes, Sir . . .

HOLMES. (*Hitting the clock.*) Not you . . . *him!*

BRIGHTON. Yes, Sir.

HOLMES. Brighton, I must have a word with you . . . in

private. (*Leading him away from the clock.*) You can do your master and me a great service.

BRIGHTON. Anything, Sir, for Sir Gilbert . . . Sir.

HOLMES. Move freely about the house. Observe everything . . . and report to me at intervals. *Long* intervals.

BRIGHTON. Yes, Sir.

HOLMES. (*Gathering up his satchels.*) And, Brighton, show amazement at nothing which might occur.

BRIGHTON. Very well, Sir. No amazement.

HOLMES. Good man, Brighton. (*Exit.*)

BRIGHTON. Thank you, Sir. (*Crosses to the clock and begins to wipe the polished wooden case.*)

WATSON. (*Entering—disguised as* MRS. ALAN.) Holmes! Holmes! I've just made a remarkable discovery! (*Cross to* BRIGHTON.) Holmes . . . ?

BRIGHTON. (*Showing no amazement.*) As you will, Sir.

(*The clock strikes the quarter-hour—11:15.*)

WATSON. What a remarkable disguise!

BRIGHTON. Thank you, Sir.

WATSON. Not you! The grandfather clock!

BRIGHTON. (*Backing away, but showing no amazement.*) I see, Sir. Yes, Sir.

WATSON. (*Crossing to clock.*) That *is* you, isn't it, Holmes?

SIR SULLIVAN. (*Speaking in* HOLMES'S *voice from within the clock.*) Go away!

WATSON. Yes . . . Of course . . . (*In cracked falsetto pidgin English to* BRIGHTON.) I . . . I . . . Uh . . . I go see about dinner.

BRIGHTON. Of course, Sir.

WATSON. (*To the clock.*) Fooled him completely! (*Exit.*)

SIR GILBERT. (*Entering at another door with a carpetbag.*) Oh, there you are, Brighton . . .

BRIGHTON. (*Helping with the bag.*) Yes, Sir.

SIR GILBERT. As you may have noticed, we are presently experiencing something of an irregular situation in the household.

BRIGHTON. (*Glancing at the clock.*) Irregular, Sir? I hadn't noticed, Sir.

SIR GILBERT. At such times, we all must make sacrifices.

BRIGHTON. Naturally, Sir.

SIR GILBERT. (*Pulling a quick-change cook's costume from the carpet-bag.*) Put this on.

BRIGHTON. But, Sir . . .

SIR GILBERT. It's a sacrifice.

BRIGHTON. Indeed it is, Sir. (*Putting on the costume, which disguises him as* MRS. ALAN, *the cook.*)

SIR GILBERT. Not that Sherlock Holmes is incapable of dealing with our current "irregularities" unaided . . . But as a practical matter, I believe in diversifying my investments. You, Brighton, are a diversification.

BRIGHTON. Thank you, Sir.

SIR GILBERT. Your disguise is but a part of a plan which I am presently devising. Mind you, the plan is not complete. At present it is . . . lucidly unformed.

BRIGHTON. Might I make a suggestion, Sir?

SIR GILBERT. I would consider it.

BRIGHTON. If it is acceptable to you, Sir, I could move freely about the house . . . observe everything . . . and report to you at intervals.

SIR GILBERT. Capital! Capital! See that you do just that! (BRIGHTON *crosses to door.*) Oh . . . and while you're about that, would you mind setting up the traditional festive ornamental archway with decorations for the New Year?

BRIGHTON. Not at all, Sir.

SIR GILBERT. Higher, Brighton. In character . . .

BRIGHTON. (*Reluctantly in a cracked falsetto.*) Not at all, Sir.

SIR GILBERT. Take every care with the ornamental archway. I am very fond of it. The loss of it would pain me greatly for it is quite valuable.

BRIGHTON. Yes, Sir.

SIR GILBERT. Now I must devise a plan or so to help Mr. Holmes. Go and do whatever it was you said.

BRIGHTON. Move . . . Observe . . . Report . . . Sir.

SIR GILBERT. Whatever . . . That will be all.

BRIGHTON. Yes, Sir. (*Exit.*)

SIR GILBERT. (*Searching the desk.*) I cannot believe that the recipe has been stolen. Perhaps it slipped down behind a drawer. I must find the secret recipe for Licorice Marshmallows! (*At the magic phrase, "Licorice Marshmallows," SIR SULLIVAN, still disguised as MRS. ALAN, and closely resembling BRIGHTON disguised as MRS. ALAN, pops out of the grandfather clock and creeps up behind SIR GILBERT, his fingers clutching in gleeful anticipation of possession of the priceless recipe.*) Aha . . . What is this? (*Reaching behind a drawer.*) I have it . . . No, I dropped it . . . A little farther . . . Ahh . . . Almost . . . Oh, drat! Perhaps I can reach it with the fire tongs. (*SIR GILBERT crosses to the fireplace. SIR SULLIVAN dives for the desk, plunges his arm into the drawer and plucks out a thick envelope. SIR GILBERT returning to the desk.*) Brighton! What are you doing here in that curiously semi-recumbent position?

SIR SULLIVAN. (*In his own voice.*) I have it!

SIR GILBERT. (*Indicating his throat.*) No, no. Higher . . . higher! (*SIR SULLIVAN without thinking, raises the envelope higher. SIR GILBERT takes it from his fingers.*) Thank you, Brighton. I have been looking for this.

SIR SULLIVAN. (*Snatching the envelope.*) And I have found it!

SIR GILBERT. (*Snatching it back.*) And I am most grateful!

SIR SULLIVAN. (*Snatching it back.*) I shall have this . . . or know the reason why.

SIR GILBERT. (*Snatching the envelope back and holding it up out of reach in the fireplace tongs.*) Because I won't give it to you . . . That's why! (*Sternly.*) Brighton, this isn't like you at all!

SIR SULLIVAN. Give me that envelope! (*They begin a chase around the desk.*)

SIR GILBERT. I certainly will not!

SIR SULLIVAN. Will too!

SIR GILBERT. Will not! Brighton, you forget yourself! (*Darting around the desk and tugging at the bell cord.*) Help! Help! Mad Butler! Mad Butler!

(*The door flies open. HOLMES enters in his Cantonese Salad-Chef disguise. The Mandarin beard and moustache on an elastic string, and the chef's hat with Oriental queue sewn on are reasonably convincing. The outsized metal mixing-bowl and large tin spoon he carries are a clever touch. But HOLMES still wears his Inverness cape, which gives the game away. HOLMES beats on the bowl to punctuate his remarks and, to his mind, firmly establish his character as a manic Mandarin kitchen-menial.*)

HOLMES. (*In awful Pidgin English.*) You lang, Sir? (*Beating the bowl.*) Lingy-lingy-lingy. I you new salad-chef. I makee salad chop-chop. Chop-chop best way to makee salad! (*Beats the bowl and skips about with short music-hall oriental steps.*)

SIR GILBERT. Mr. Holmes . . . !

SIR SULLIVAN. (*Dropping instantly into the role of MRS. ALAN.*) Mr. Holmes . . . !

HOLMES. (*Whipping off his disguise.*) Do not be alarmed. In reality, it is I . . . Sherlock Holmes. That was but another of my impenetrable disguises.

SIR GILBERT. This . . . "person" . . . attacked me! Attempted to seize this valuable parcel from my very hands!

HOLMES. (*Crossing to* SIR SULLIVAN.) No doubt from an excess of good intentions. Not to worry. (*Nudging* SIR SULLIVAN.) Restraint, Watson . . . restraint.

SIR SULLIVAN. (*As* MRS. ALAN.) Yes . . . Oh, yes . . . Sir.

HOLMES. I assure you that this "person" meant no harm.

SIR GILBERT. Do you know what is in this envelope, Holmes? Do you know its value?

HOLMES. Of course I do. But I suppose that it would give you great pleasure to announce that you have found the missing recipe for Licorice Marshmallows.

SIR GILBERT. It would indeed . . . But I haven't.

SIR SULLIVAN. (*Distressed . . . Yea, foiled.*) Oh . . . ?

SIR GILBERT. This is my collection of stereopticon slides of Queen Victoria and Prince Albert at the Crystal Palace. It has been a great inconvenience to have been without them all these years.

HOLMES. Oh . . . Well . . . I expected as much. But this is time neither to dilly nor to dally. We must go about our daily business duly. Go. Prepare for the festivities. Time is short!

SIR GILBERT. Of course. Come, Brighton.

HOLMES. Go, Watson.

SIR GILBERT. (*At the door, turning.*) Watson . . . ?!

HOLMES. Brighton . . . ?!

ALL THREE. Mrs. Alan!

(SIR GILBERT *and the disguised* SIR SULLIVAN *exit.*)

HOLMES. (*Examining his Cantonese salad-chef disguise.*) Mmm . . . Perhaps a *red* beard and dark glasses would do the trick. (*The grandfather clock strikes the half-hour—11:30.* HOLMES *crosses to the clock.*) Watson . . . ? (*Opens clock and peers inside.*) I thought not.

(*There is a noise at the door.* HOLMES *hurries to the oppo-site door. There is a sound at that door too.* HOLMES *hides behind the draperies. Two mysterious figures in black hooded capes enter from opposite sides of the room. They meet and embrace, then throw off the capes.*)

BERTRAM. Lucy . . .

LUCY. Bertram . . .

BERTRAM. It is good of you to comfort me in this, my saddest and possibly final hour.

LUCY. It's the least I can do.

BERTRAM. Yes, I know. But one must make do.

LUCY. I thought that if you could pour out your sorrow to a friendly ear, you would feel better.

BERTRAM. You do have friendly ears.

LUCY. You had better pour quickly. It's already eleven thirty-two.

BERTRAM. Eleven thirty-four. I'd best get on with the pouring.

BERTRAM'S CLOCKWORK SONG

BERTRAM. (*Singing.*)
Mourn, mourn the closing year
  For Clockwork Bertram Mallow.
I show a good face,
  But in my watch-case,
My river of time runs shallow.

BERTRAM and LUCY.
I show ⎱
He shows ⎰ a good face,
  But in his ⎱ watch-case,
      my ⎰
My ⎱
His ⎰ river of time runs shallow.

BERTRAM.
Hark! Mark the festive time
  With merry birthday sounding.
Without a good wind,
  Quite shortly I'll find
My mainspring is running down . . . Ding!
  BERTRAM and LUCY.
Without a good wind,
  Quite shortly $\begin{Bmatrix} \text{I'll} \\ \text{he'll} \end{Bmatrix}$ find

$\begin{Bmatrix} \text{My} \\ \text{His} \end{Bmatrix}$ mainspring is running down . . . Ding!
  BERTRAM.
Strike, strike the happy hour,
  And savour the seconds in it.
It's a matter of time
  'Til my Westminster chime
Will not even strike the minute!

(HOLMES *slips from his hiding place and, holding his hands in benediction over the heads of* BERTRAM *and* LUCY, *softly joins them in the final refrain.*)

BERTRAM, LUCY and HOLMES.
It's a matter of time
  'Til $\begin{Bmatrix} \text{my} \\ \text{his} \end{Bmatrix}$ Westminster chime
Will not even strike the minute!
  HOLMES. (*Applauding softly.*) Bravo!
  LUCY. (*Startled.*) We are undone!
  BERTRAM. (*Startled.*) I am unwound!
  HOLMES. Not to fear. I wish only to enlist your aid in my master plan to unwind this mystery and run down the culprit.
  BERTRAM. Oh . . . that's all right then.
  LUCY. What can I do to help?

HOLMES. (*To* LUCY.) I congratulate you upon your stead-fastness. Bertram, your only salvation lies in practicing an outrageous deception which I have devised.

BERTRAM. How long do I have to practice this deception?

HOLMES. Until you get it right. I think . . . first . . . a disguise.

BERTRAM. What sort of disguise?

HOLMES. An *impenetrable* disguise. Hark! Someone is coming. Look inconspicuous!

(*They all dart to different parts of the room.* LUCY *dusts the sideboard.* BERTRAM *becomes terribly interested in the snow-storm paperweight.* HOLMES *devotes consider-able attention to a close examination of the mantel. The total effect is, unfortunately, terribly conspicuous. The hall doors open.* BRIGHTON, *disguised as* MRS. ALAN, *struggles in with the traditional festive cere-monial archway. It is an ornate three-fold screen, the middle section of which is covered with a roller blind bearing appropriate sentiments for the celebration of the New Year.*)

BRIGHTON. (*As* MRS. ALAN.) Excuse me, but I must set up the traditional festive ceremonial archway. (*He carries it to the Center of the room.*)

HOLMES. (*Spuriously casual.*) Why, look who's here. It's Mrs. Alan, the cook. That's Mrs. Alan, isn't it! Let's all help Mrs. Alan set up the traditional festive ceremonial archway.

BRIGHTON. Thank you, Sir.

(*They help set up the archway.*)

HOLMES. We must go now, Mrs. Alan. Let's all say goodbye to Mrs. Alan. Goodbye, Mrs. Alan. (*Whispers.*) Good man, Watson. Fooled them completely. (*Cross to door.*)

BERTRAM. Goodbye . . . Mrs. Alan . . . ? (*Cross to door*.)

LUCY. Goodbye, Mrs. Alan.

BRIGHTON. (*Softly but sternly to* LUCY.) That's Mrs. Alan, *SIR*.

LUCY. (*Puzzled*.) Goodbye, Mrs. Alan, Sir.

HOLMES. Come, come. (*As they go*.) I have this splendid Cantonese Salad-Chef disguise which is absolutely impenetrable . . . Well . . . *almost* absolutely impenetrable.

BERTRAM. Last year I got a fireman suit for my birthday.

HOLMES. We shall see . . .

(ALL *exit except* BRIGHTON *in his* MRS. ALAN *disguise. As they go out,* WATSON, *disguised as* MRS. ALAN, *toddles in unnoticed from the opposite side. He notices the archway and approaches it from the side opposite* BRIGHTON. *Simultaneously both bend down and raise the window-blind so that the center section is an open doorway.* MIRROR MUSIC *begins.* BRIGHTON *and* WATSON *mistake each other for mirror reflections. They look, adjust their wigs, straighten their aprons, step toward and away from the "mirror," dance past it, polish the "mirror" then, nose to nose, circle each other through the opening. Suddenly it occurs to them that something is very wrong with this mirror. With one final startled look at each other, they run off in opposite directions, calling for help.* MIRROR MUSIC *ends*.)

BRIGHTON and WATSON. (*Running out*.) Holmes! Mr. Holmes! Mr. Holmes!

(*From another door,* SIR SULLIVAN, *also disguised as* MRS. ALAN, *runs in, quickly folds the screen and, chuckling with evil glee, dashes with it to the hall doors. The hall doors are flung open.* SIR SULLIVAN *runs off in the other direction with the archway. The CLOCK*

STRIKES the three-quarter hour—11:45. SIR GILBERT marches solemnly into the drawing room and stands at the head of the table.)

SIR GILBERT. Since he's running down at midnight, we're starting the celebration early.

(He strikes a single sad note on a crystal goblet. The RUNNING DOWN BIRTHDAY SONG *begins. It is a majestic dirge. The* MAIDS *march slowly in with trays of food.* LUCY *carries a small birthday cake with a single brave burning candle on it.* BERTRAM *marches in and takes his place at the table.* HOLMES *marches in and joins them.* HOLMES *is now disguised in a bright . . . yea, blazing red full beard and dark glasses, but he still wears his deerstalker cap and Inverness cape. Everyone puts on unconvincingly merry paper hats. Glasses are filled for the toast, but as they sing, all but* HOLMES *dissolve into tears. Handkerchiefs are much in evidence.*

THE RUNNING-DOWN BIRTHDAY SONG

MAIDS.
Mourn, mourn the closing year
  For Clockwork Bertram Mallow.
He shows a good face,
  But in his watch-case,
His river of time runs shallow.
  ALL BUT BERTRAM.
He shows a good face,
  But in his watch-case,
His river of time runs shallow.
  MAIDS.
Hark! Mark the festive time
  With merry birthday sounding.

Without a good wind,
Quite shortly he'll find
His mainspring is running down . . . Ding!
ALL BUT BERTRAM.
Without a good wind,
Quite shortly he'll find
His mainspring is running down . . . Ding!
MAIDS.
Strike, strike the happy hour,
And savour the seconds in it.
It's a matter of time
'Til his Westminster chime
Will not even strike the minute!
ALL BUT BERTRAM.
It's a matter of time
'Til his Westminster chime
Will not even strike the minute!

(*The grandfather clock begins to strike the hour of midnight.*)

SIR GILBERT. (*Stands and raises his glass.*) To the Queen
. . . To the New Century . . . To Clockwork Bertram
Mallow . . .

BERTRAM. (*Rising, as does* HOLMES.) To the Queen
. . . To the New Century . . . To Clockwork . . .
(*Slowing.*) Bert . . . ram . . . Mall . . . (*On the last
stroke of midnight.*) ow . . .

(BERTRAM *runs to a full stop and stands like a store-window
mannekin. The* MAIDS *pick him up and carry him out
like a statue.* HOLMES *goes to the grandfather clock
and opens the front to investigate.*)

SIR GILBERT. (*In a frenzy of grief and a paper hat.*)
Lost . . . lost . . . lost . . . Bertram . . . my Clockwork Prince . . . Bertram . . . my son . . . !

(*In his distraction and grief,* SIR GILBERT *shoves the door of the clock shut, locking* HOLMES *inside.* SIR GILBERT *crosses to the table, blows out the single candle on the birthday cake and sinks into a chair, his head in his hands.* WATSON, *disguised as* MRS. ALAN, *rushes into the drawing room.*)

WATSON. Holmes! Holmes! I heard the clock strike . . . and I saw them carrying young Bertram out . . . stiff as a mackerel! And I . . . ! Oh . . . Sorry, Sir Gilbert . . .

SIR GILBERT. Mrs. Alan, your sympathetic expressions of grief are greatly appreciated. Please be silent and leave me to my sad memories . . .

WATSON. (*Mumbling.*) Oh, yes . . . certainly . . . I quite understand . . . (*Sits off to one side of the room.*)

BRIGHTON. (*Rushing into the room from another door, still disguised as* MRS. ALAN.) Sir Gilbert! I heard the clock strike . . . and I saw them carrying young Bertram out . . . !

SIR GILBERT. (*Slightly annoyed by the apparent repetition.*) Yes, yes, I know! Mackerel and all that. Now please *do* be silent and leave me to my sad memories!

BRIGHTON. Yes, Sir. Very good, Sir. (*Sits, not noticing* WATSON.)

SIR SULLIVAN. (*Rushing in from yet another door, still disguised as* MRS. ALAN.) Sir Gilbert! I heard the clock strike . . . !

SIR GILBERT. (*Postively irritated.*) I *know!* Carrying out! Mackerel! Why on earth can't you be *silent!* You are confusing my sad memories!

SIR SULLIVAN. (*As* MRS. ALAN.) Yes . . . yes . . . Oh, yes, Sir. (*Sits, not noticing* WATSON *and* BRIGHTON.)

SIR GILBERT. (*Pulling himself together.*) Such undisguised grief is not the British way. (*Rises and speaks to each of the* MESDAMES ALAN *in turn . . . with growing realization that he is seeing triple.*) Mrs. Alan . . . Mrs. Alan . . . ? Mrs. Alan . . . !!

WATSON, BRIGHTON and SIR SULLIVAN. (*Noticing each other for the first time and rising.*) Mrs. Alan . . . ?!

SIR GILBERT. (*Dumbfounded.*) Ohh . . . I . . . Sir Gilbert Mallow . . . The Marshmallow King . . . have indeed gone *crackers!*

(*The hall doors burst open to reveal* BERTRAM, *disguised as* HOLMES *in disguise.* BERTRAM *wears the cape, deer-stalker cap, blazing red beard and dark glasses. He does a rather good impersonation of* HOLMES, *although he would have preferred a Fireman suit.*)

BERTRAM. (*As* HOLMES.) The trap is sprung!

SIR GILBERT. Don't talk about springs when I've gone crackers! (*Gesturing at the collection of* ALANS.)

BERTRAM. Contain yourself, Sir Gilbert. The real Mrs. Alan could not have heard the clock strike the fateful hour. She can't hear *thunder!* Therefore it stands to reason that one of these persons is *not* the real Mrs. Alan!

SIR GILBERT. Quite so, Mr. Holmes.

BERTRAM. Indeed, it is most likely that *two* of them are not the real Mrs. Alan!

SIR GILBERT. What logic!

BERTRAM. (*Crossing to* BRIGHTON.) In fact, this almost impenetrable disguise conceals my faithful friend and companion, Dr. John Watson! (BERTRAM *whips off the white wig and bit of flannel about the throat to reveal* BRIGHTON.) Oh . . . It's you, Brighton.

BRIGHTON. (*Climbing out of the quick-change costume.*) Dreadfully sorry, Sir.

WATSON. (*Chuckling as he takes off his* MRS. ALAN *disguise.*) Fooled you that time, Holmes. And . . . *and* . . . in spite of your current impenetrable disguise, I recognized *you* immediately!

BERTRAM. (*Still as* HOLMES.) Then through the process of elimination and the exercise of logic . . . (*Indicating* SIR SULLIVAN.) This is the real Mrs. Alan.

SIR SULLIVAN. (*In a cracked falsetto, backing toward the clock.*) Yes . . . yes . . . Oh, yes, Sir. And a happy new year to you too, Sir.

HOLMES. (*Stepping out of the clock in his red beard and dark glasses.*) A happy new year, indeed! (HOLMES *pulls off* SIR SULLIVAN's *wig and bit of flannel.*) The game is up!

SIR SULLIVAN. (*Whipping off his quick-change costume to stand revealed in his full-dress suit and black waxed moustache. He places his monocle in his eye.*) Yes . . . It is I!

SIR GILBERT. I suppose it is. Who *are* you?

WATSON. Never saw him before in my life. (*To* BERTRAM.) You know him, Holmes?

BERTRAM. (*As* HOLMES.) Perfect stranger to me.

SIR SULLIVAN. You have unmasked me . . . But . . . (*Pointing at* BERTRAM.) at least I have the satisfaction of having defeated the famous Mr. Sherlock Holmes! (*To* HOLMES.) May I have the honour of knowing the name of my worthy opponent?

HOLMES. You may call me John Robinson.

SIR SULLIVAN. Mr. Robinson, you have defeated me.

HOLMES. Or, if you prefer, you may call me . . . (*Removing his red beard and dark glasses.*) Mr. Sherlock Holmes!

SIR SULLIVAN. Oh, drat! Just . . . drat!

HOLMES. And I shall call you by your proper name . . . Sir Sullivan Sinister!

ALL. Sir Sullivan Sinister!

HOLMES. Put the derbies on him, Watson.

WATSON. I didn't wear my derby . . . If I'd known . . .

HOLMES. Derbies, Watson! Derbies! Handcuffs.

WATSON. (*Handcuffing* SIR SULLIVAN.) Yes . . . Yes, of course. I was just funning.

SIR GILBERT. (*Indicating* BERTRAM, *who is disguised as* HOLMES.) Then who is this?

BERTRAM. (*Taking off the red beard, dark glasses, deer-stalker cap and cloak.*) I am Bertram, your son!

SIR GILBERT. Can I believe my eyes! But you . . .

BERTRAM. I told you I could do Westminster chimes. (*He presses his ear and chimes a sample.*)

SIR GILBERT. (*Embracing him.*) My son!

BERTRAM. I chimed midnight . . . early. All part of the plan.

SIR SULLIVAN. (*To* HOLMES.) Still I am triumphant! You have not found the *key* to the mystery . . . and to Clockwork Bertram Mallow!

HOLMES. Haven't I just! ''The key to the mystery hides in the locks.'' You thought that would be too great a puzzle for me! I know of your passion for logical symmetry and bad puns . . .

SIR SULLIVAN. You know! He knows!

HOLMES. I know. Here, in the white locks of this wig, is hidden . . . Bertram Mallow's Large Brass Key!

SIR GILBERT. We are saved . . . saved . . . *saved!*

HOLMES. (*Winding* BERTRAM *up.*) As I always say . . . one good turn deserves another.

BERTRAM. I feel so much better now.

HOLMES. (*Giving key to* SIR GILBERT.) See that you keep this large brass key in a safe place until next year. I might be out of town.

(*The grandfather clock really begins to strike midnight.*)

SIR GILBERT. Stop that, Bertram.

BERTRAM. That isn't me. It's really the clock. Happy New Year!

SIR GILBERT. Bertram . . . now you are a man. You should be self-winding. (*Gives him the key.*)

HOLMES. (*Flinging wide the hall doors.*) Let us truly welcome the new year . . . 1900! Let us truly welcome the New Century.

(*The* MAIDS *enter, wheeling a tea-trolly with a giant birthday cake upon it.* LUCY *rushes to embrace* BERTRAM.
*Outside, Big Ben rings in the New Century. Shouts,
sirens, ship's horns, bells and fireworks herald the
New Century.* ALL *put on funny paper hats and blow
on little paper horns.*)

SIR GILBERT. (*Silencing them.*) One moment! At this
festive time, I must inquire . . . where is our faithful
cook, Mrs. Alan?

(*There is a stir as each looks at the other to pose the question, but there is no immediate answer.*)

HOLMES. (*Crossing to the gigantic cake.*) If I deduce
correctly from the ear-trumpet protruding from the center
of this Christmas Pantomime birthday cake . . . I have
found your Mrs. Alan. (*Shouting into the cake.*) Happy
New Year!

(MRS. ALAN *bursts through the paper top of the cake,
dressed as Britannia, waving a Union Jack and holding aloft an orange-striped tabby-cat.*)

MRS. ALAN. (*The* real MRS. ALAN.) Long live the cat!

(ALL *cheer.*)

SIR GILBERT. Mrs. Alan, I appreciate your sincere efforts
to enhance our celebration, but what are you doing in that
cake?
MRS. ALAN. It is, isn't it! But you said, "Stay home and
hide in the baker's treat."
SIR GILBERT. I sent your for *Holmes* . . . to find him in
Baker Street! *Baker Street!*
MRS. ALAN. You're entirely welcome, Sir. Here's the
menu for dinner.
HOLMES. (*Unrolling the menu.*) Just as I thought. On this

side . . . the menu. On *this* side . . . the secret recipe for Licorice Marshmallows!

SIR GILBERT. We are saved . . . saved . . . saved! Bertram, this is yours! (*Gives him the recipe.*)

BERTRAM. Marshmallows forever!

SIR SULLIVAN. It should have been *mine!*

SIR GILBERT. Oh, hush. But Mr. Holmes, how did you know?

HOLMES. A minor exercise in logic. Who better than a cook to have a recipe?

WATSON. Jove, Holmes . . . you are the most perfect reasoning and observing machine that the world has seen!

HOLMES. (*Raising a glass.*) A toast to the New Century . . .

ALL. (*Raising glasses.*) To the New Century . . .

HOLMES. To the Brave New World that has . . . (*Slower.*) such people . . . in . . . (HOLMES—*yes,* HOLMES—*is running down!*) Quick, Watson . . . the . . . key . . . (WATSON *dives for the proper compartment in his satchel, brings out a Large Brass Key and winds* HOLMES *up.* HOLMES, *totally recovered and good as new.*) To the Brave New World, that has such people in it! To Good Queen Victoria . . . To the New Century . . . To the Clockwork Prince . . . And to us all!

ALL. (*Drinking the toast.*) To the Clockwork Prince . . . and to us all!

(*The MUSIC of the* FINALE *begins to play.* BERTRAM *dances with* LUCY. SIR GILBERT *dances with* MRS. ALAN. BRIGHTON *and* WATSON *dance with* MELISSA *and* JANE. SIR SULLIVAN *sulks morose and vengeful in handcuffs and the corner.* HOLMES *whips out his violin and accompanies the dance round. In the streets of London, fireworks, church bells, sirens, horns, whistles and cheering throngs welcome the New Century!*)

CURTAIN

PROPERTY PLOT

Set Props:
papers, envelopes and pencils in and on desk
bell cord by main doorway
spring bell Offstage in main hallway
large brass key in tin box in desk
decanters and glasses on sideboard
small box with tiny lock on desk
snow-storm glass paperweight on desk
fire-tongs beside fireplace
decorative archway Offstage—brought on by BRIGHTON
portrait of Queen Victoria over mantel
giant birthday cake on tea trolly Offstage—brought on by
      MAIDS

Hand Props:
pocket watch (BRIGHTON)
feather dusters, dust cloths, mops, brooms and buckets
      (MAIDS)
birthday and New Year's Eve decorations (MAIDS)
ear trumpet (MRS. ALAN)
satchel of burglar tools and explosives (SIR SULLIVAN)
ransom note (SIR SULLIVAN)
small cat funeral wreath with black ribbons (MRS. ALAN)
assorted keys (SERVANTS)
satchels and portmanteaus (WATSON)
calling cards (WATSON)
satchel and violin in case (HOLMES)
large scrapbook (WATSON)
pipe and magnifying glass (HOLMES)
note from SIR SULLIVAN (HOLMES)
large brass key in satchel (WATSON)
pocket notebook and pencil (WATSON)

carpet bag (SIR GILBERT)
large metal mixing bowl and tin spoon (HOLMES)
trays of party food and drink (MAIDS)
small birthday cake (LUCY)
paper hats and paper horns (MAIDS)
handkerchiefs (ALL)
handcuffs (WATSON)
Union Jack flag (MRS. ALAN)
orange-striped tabby-cat (MRS. ALAN)

SHERLOCK HOLMES AND THE CURIOUS ADVENTURE OF THE CLOCKWORK PRINCE

HALL BACKING

PROSCENIUM

ROOM BACKING

FIREPLACE

ROOM BACKING

CHAIR

CHAIR

CHAIR

HASSOCK

SLIDING DOOR

CHAIR

BELL CORD

GRANDFATHER CLOCK

CHAIR

CHAIR

CHAIR

TABLE

CHAIR

CHAIR

SLIDING DOOR

SIDEBOARD

CHAIR

DESK

ROOM BACKING

CHAIR

OUTSIDE HOUSE WALL

FRENCH DOORS

LONDON NIGHT-SCENE BACKING

RAILING

CHAIR

FRONT CURTAIN

TREASURE ISLAND
Ken Ludwig

All Groups / Adventure / 10m, 1f (doubling) / Areas
Based on the masterful adventure novel by Robert Louis Steven-
son, *Treasure Island* is a stunning yarn of piracy on the tropical
seas. It begins at an inn on the Devon coast of England in 1775
and quickly becomes an unforgettable tale of treachery and
mayhem featuring a host of legendary swashbucklers including
the dangerous Billy Bones (played unforgettably in the movies
by Lionel Barrymore), the sinister two-timing Israel Hands, the
brassy woman pirate Anne Bonney, and the hideous form of evil
incarnate, Blind Pew. At the center of it all are Jim Hawkins, a
14-year-old boy who longs for adventure, and the infamous Long
John Silver, who is a complex study of good and evil, perhaps the
most famous hero-villain of all time. Silver is an unscrupulous
buccaneer-rogue whose greedy quest for gold, coupled with his
affection for Jim, cannot help but win the heart of every soul
who has ever longed for romance, treasure and adventure.

SKIN DEEP
Jon Lonoff

Comedy / 2m, 2f / Interior Unit Set

In *Skin Deep*, a large, lovable, lonely-heart, named Maureen Mulligan, gives romance one last shot on a blind-date with sweet awkward Joseph Spinelli; she's learned to pepper her speech with jokes to hide insecurities about her weight and appearance, while he's almost dangerously forthright, saying everything that comes to his mind. They both know they're perfect for each other, and in time they come to admit it.

They were set up on the date by Maureen's sister Sheila and her husband Squire, who are having problems of their own: Sheila undergoes a non-stop series of cosmetic surgeries to hang onto the attractive and much-desired Squire, who may or may not have long ago held designs on Maureen, who introduced him to Sheila. With Maureen particularly vulnerable to both hurting and being hurt, the time is ripe for all these unspoken issues to bubble to the surface.

"Warm-hearted comedy … the laughter was literally show-stopping. A winning play, with enough good-humored laughs and sentiment to keep you smiling from beginning to end."
– *TalkinBroadway.com*

"It's a little Paddy Chayefsky, a lot Neil Simon and a quick-witted, intelligent voyage into the not-so-tranquil seas of middle-aged love and dating. The dialogue is crackling and hilarious; the plot simple but well-turned; the characters endearing and quirky; and lurking beneath the merriment is so much heartache that you'll stand up and cheer when the unlikely couple makes it to the inevitable final clinch."
– *NYTheatreWorld.Com*

COCKEYED
William Missouri Downs

Comedy / 3m, 1f / Unit Set

Phil, an average nice guy, is madly in love with the beautiful Sophia. The only problem is that she's unaware of his existence. He tries to introduce himself but she looks right through him. When Phil discovers Sophia has a glass eye, he thinks that might be the problem, but soon realizes that she really can't see him. Perhaps he is caught in a philosophical hyperspace or dualistic reality or perhaps beautiful women are just unaware of nice guys. Armed only with a B.A. in philosophy, Phil sets out to prove his existence and win Sophia's heart. This fast moving farce is the winner of the HotCity Theatre's GreenHouse New Play Festival. The St. Louis Post-Dispatch called Cockeyed a clever romantic comedy, Talkin' Broadway called it "hilarious," while Playback Magazine said that it was "fresh and invigorating."

Winner!
of the HotCity Theatre GreenHouse New Play Festival

"Rocking with laughter...hilarious...polished and engaging work draws heavily on the age-old conventions of farce: improbable situations, exaggerated characters, amazing coincidences, absurd misunderstandings, people hiding in closets and barely missing each other as they run in and out of doors...full of comic momentum as Cockeyed hurtles toward its conclusion."
–Talkin' Broadway

ANON
Kate Robin

Drama / 2m, 12f / Area

Anon. follows two couples as they cope with sexual addiction. Trip and Allison are young and healthy, but he's more interested in his abnormally large porn collection than in her. While they begin to work through both of their own sexual and relationship hang-ups, Trip's parents are stuck in the roles they've been carving out for years in their dysfunctional marriage. In between scenes with these four characters, 10 different women, members of a support group for those involved with individuals with sex addiction issues, tell their stories in monologues that are alternately funny and harrowing..

In addition to Anon., Robin's play What They Have was also commissioned by South Coast Repertory. Her plays have also been developed at Manhattan Theater Club, Playwrights Horizons, New York Theatre Workshop, The Eugene O'Neill Theater Center's National Playwrights Conference, JAW/West at Portland Center Stage and Ensemble Studio Theatre. Television and film credits include "Six Feet Under" (writer/supervising producer) and "Coming Soon." Robin received the 2003 Princess Grace Statuette for playwriting and is an alumna of New Dramatists.

WHITE BUFFALO
Don Zolidis

Drama / 3m, 2f (plus chorus)/ Unit Set

Based on actual events, WHITE BUFFALO tells the story of the miracle birth of a white buffalo calf on a small farm in southern Wisconsin. When Carol Gelling discovers that one of the buffalo on her farm is born white in color, she thinks nothing more of it than a curiosity. Soon, however, she learns that this is the fulfillment of an ancient prophecy believed by the Sioux to bring peace on earth and unity to all mankind. Her little farm is quickly overwhelmed with religious pilgrims, bringing her into contact with a culture and faith that is wholly unfamiliar to her. When a mysterious businessman offers to buy the calf for two million dollars, Carol is thrown into doubt about whether to profit from the religious beliefs of others or to keep true to a spirituality she knows nothing about.